An Indian Adventure

Stories linking with the History
National Curriculum Key Stage 2

First published in 1998 by Franklin Watts
as Sparks: The Great Raj

This paperback edition published in 1999

Franklin Watts
96 Leonard Street
London EC2A 4XD

Franklin Watts Australia
14 Mars Road
Lane Cove
NSW 2066

Editor: Matthew Parselle
Series Editor: Paula Borton
Designer: Kirstie Billingham
Consultant: Dr Anne Millard, BA Hons, Dip Ed, PhD

A CIP catalogue record for this book
is available from the British Library.

ISBN 0 7496 3451 0 (pbk)
        0 7496 3090 6 (hbk)

Dewey Classification 954.03

Printed in Great Britain

An Indian Adventure

by
Mary Hooper

Illustrations by Greg Gormley

W
FRANKLIN WATTS
NEW YORK • LONDON • SYDNEY

1

A Bit of a Do

Lucy woke early and felt hot and cross straight away. She scratched her arm – another mosquito bite! The nasty little beast must have somehow got through the muslin curtain which was draped over her bed. She scratched her way up her arm.

No, it wasn't a
mosquito bite, it was
prickly heat – a horribly irritating rash
which came up when it thought it would
and which she'd never had in England.
She now had it, she realised, up one arm,
across her shoulders, and down the other.
Today of all days!

Lucy scratched and wriggled furiously.
She knew prickly heat from old, knew that
however much calamine lotion she

splashed on, it would stay itchy, red and infuriating all day. Lucy grimaced to herself – and wouldn't she look fine with sore, pink arms sticking out of her new long white silk dress? The special dress that her mother had made such a fuss about and had sent to England to have made.

As the rising sun hit the wooden shutters of the room the first wave of the day's heat passed across it, and Lucy heaved a sigh.

She would never get used to the heat in India. Never. And although it meant being parted from her family, she couldn't wait to go back to England and to boarding school. She really should have gone home a couple of years ago, but she'd got scarlet fever quite badly and her mother hadn't wanted her to do the long, tiring sea journey back until she was strong enough.

Lucy sat up, pulled across the muslin netting and swung her legs out of bed.

The bed swung with her. It was a type of hammock, a thin carpet-like fabric hung on knotted ropes. This, Lucy's mother had decided, was cooler than an ordinary bed and mattress. And more hygienic, too, because the fleas and tics had nowhere to burrow into.

The moment Lucy's feet touched the marble tiled floor there was a movement from outside and the ayah, Lucy's nursemaid, appeared.

"Good morning, Missy!" Her ayah was a young Indian woman, dressed that day in a lime-green silk sari.

"Morning," Lucy mumbled, still half asleep. That was another thing she'd never get used to – the number of servants in the house. In England there had been maids, but here in India there were servants to do everything. You couldn't move without a servant asking you if you wanted anything,

or brushing the ground in front of you, or
just standing around in case you wanted a
door opened, or a drink poured, or even –
as Lucy had once seen – a page turned
over in the book you were reading. If you
stayed in India for long, Lucy thought,
then you'd lose the ability to do anything
for yourself!

"Special day today," the ayah said.
"All up early!"

Lucy nodded, going into the bathroom
and shutting the door behind her.

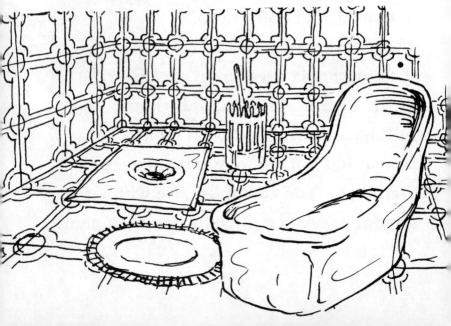

The bathroom was a beautifully tiled room with a hole in one corner that was used as a loo, and a tin bath, and here, at least, she could be on her own.

"Special day!" the ayah sung from behind the door. "You look lovely today!"
Lucy pulled a face.
She doubted that.
She would probably
look like a lobster in
a frock. Everyone else
would look splendid,
though, for it was
a special occasion.

It was New Year's Day, 1877, the day that Queen Victoria was to be declared Empress of India. All over India there were to be celebrations – great, extravagant, lavish celebrations. And Lucy and her mother and father were going to

Government House in Delhi, to witness the actual declaration ceremony by Lord Lytton, the Viceroy of India. Lucy even had a very tiny part in it – she had to present a posy of flowers to one of the great men taking part.

"You want water, Missy?" the ayah called.

"Yes, please!" Lucy said. She opened the bathroom door and two servants, the water-wallahs as they were called, came in carrying giant pitchers of water which they poured into the tin bath.

It took them six

journeys each before the bath was half full
of cool water, and before Lucy got in the
ayah added some
soothing lotion to try
and calm Lucy's
prickly heat. By the
time she got out
of the bath she
felt a little less
hot and a little
less grumpy.

The bath was emptied down the hole in
the corner of the room, and Lucy went
back into her bedroom to get dressed. The
sun was beating down on the shutters of

her bedroom now, and, despite the efforts
of a punkah-wallah – the servant seated
outside on the verandah continually
pulling a rope to move
a large fan – it was
already hot and stuffy.

The ayah had laid out Lucy's best new
dress on top of one of the trunks which
stood around the room. Everything was

stored in tin trunks – not only to keep
them from getting damp in the rainy
season, but also to try and keep them out
of the way of the legions of ants and
moths. The ayah picked
up the dress and held
it towards Lucy.

"You put it on
now, or you have
chota hazri?"

"I think I'll
eat first,"
Lucy said.
Chota hazri
was breakfast,
and Lucy was
hungry. "I daren't get anything down that
dress – Mama would have a fit." She put
on a cotton wrap and went across to the
other side of the bungalow and out onto

the verandah – a wide, wooden platform
which overlooked the garden. The garden
was Lucy's mother's pride and joy – she
had plants sent from home for it.

Native Indian plants would have
grown better – and not needed half as
much water – but Lucy's mother wanted it
to be as much like an English country
garden as possible. A servant pulled out a
basket-chair and Lucy sat down just as

her father came out. He was
a high-ranking officer in the
British Army and
splendidly, if rather
hotly, dressed in full
uniform. He clapped
his hands and two
more servants
appeared, bowing.

"Tea – fast!" he
ordered. "And make it very strong.
None of your stewed up river water."
He smiled at Lucy. "A grand day, eh
what? Looking forward to it, are you?"

"Sort of," Lucy said. She was looking
forward to the big day in one way, for at
least it would mean a change from
everyday life. She'd attended official
celebrations before, though, and they
usually meant standing around for hours

listening to long speeches and then having
to make polite conversation with a lot of
old stuffed shirts.

"Good show!" said her father.
He always said that, Lucy thought to
herself, whether it was a good show or not.
She began to eat her breakfast of fruit and
rice. It might be a good show – if only
she'd stop itching...

2

India Celebrates

"Oh, how splendid!" Lucy's mother said.

"Yes. Jolly good show," said her father. And Lucy even stopped scratching her arms and let out a squeal of delight at the sight before them. The whole of Delhi, it seemed, had been decorated in Queen Victoria's honour. Buildings were festooned with flowers, flags and bunting, oil lamps and torches burned on the flat roofs of houses, and everyone – even the animals – were decked out in their brightest and their best. In the streets, thousands of people jostled for space. Most were on foot, but the wealthier were in rickshaws and carts or riding on camels or elephants. Some – like Lucy's family – were in grand carriages pulled by horses.

Lucy, not often allowed into Indian society, marvelled at it all.

"I've never seen so many people," she said. "I didn't know there were so many people in India!"

Her mother laughed. "This is just Delhi," she said. "There are celebrations in every city, every village right across the country."

"How strange," Lucy said, "all these parties in honour of Queen Victoria – and she's not even coming!"

Her mother tapped Lucy's hands to stop her scratching.

"Please," she said, "I hope you're not going to do that in front of all the important people."

"I'll try not to," Lucy said. She delved into the little silk bag which matched her

dress, and threw
a few rupees to the ragged children running
by the carriage. "I am awfully itchy,
though."

"You'll just have to sit on your hands to
stop yourself scratching, then," her mother
said. "Now, when we get to Government
House, your ayah will come and collect
you." She frowned and craned her head out
of the carriage window. "As long as they
can keep up with us in those carts, that is."

The four carts travelling behind carried
the family's servants. One held Lucy's
ayah and the ayah's assistant,

the next held
two maids for
Lucy's mother and a
small selection of her
jewels, clothes and toiletries.
The third cart carried Lucy's father's
servants, and the family cook. The fourth
held some small pieces of furniture, two
trunks of clothes and the personal
possessions the family thought they'd need
during the one night they were staying away.
The English raj never travelled lightly!

"What are we going to do all day, though?" Lucy asked.

"Oh," her mother said, "you needn't fear it'll be dull. There will be a splendid lunch, and then the proclamation will be read in front of a vast crowd. After that a party will go tiger hunting."

"I suppose we won't be allowed to go to that?" Her mother shook her head. "Of course not. The men will join us later to have a huge picnic in the hills. It's then that you'll be presenting a posy to one of the nobles."

"To Lord Lytton?" Lucy asked.

"I'm afraid not," her mother said.

"To Sir Oswald Osbert, though – he's almost as important."

Lucy nodded, by now hardly listening to her mother. There was so much going on, so many sights and sounds and smells. So many people!

Slowly, moving between lumbering elephants and rickety old carriages, between swarms of children and

spectacularly-robed princes on horseback, their carriage made its way towards Government House, where Lord Lytton, the Viceroy lived. As they pulled up at the magnificent front gates, four servants appeared to open them. The carriage made its way up the long drive towards the palace.

By the time it reached it and Lucy looked back, two other carriages were making their way up the drive. So much going on! Lucy began to get excited...

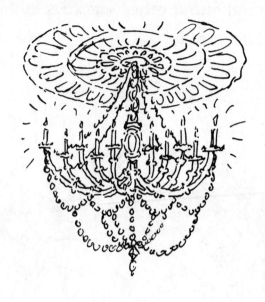

3

A Bit of a Rotter

In the vast marble entrance hall, all was confusion. As Lord Lytton's servants came to help the visitors from their carriages, the visitors' own servants, the ones they'd brought with them, rushed up to do the same thing. And they didn't like it a bit

when they found other servants looking
after their family!

Lucy, waiting for
everything to sort itself out, looked round
eagerly. From the entrance hall she could
glimpse vast open spaces – a ballroom,
a reception hall, a banqueting hall.
Each room was splendidly and lavishly
decorated in marble and gilt, with stone
pillars, great crystal chandeliers and

life-sized statues and bronzes.

"Such wealth..." Lucy's mother
murmured under her breath. Even though
she was used to wonderful houses, lavishly
furnished, this one exceeded anything she'd
seen before. A tall man in splendid red

uniform strode into the hall, his great sword clanking at his side. He was flanked by two servants, and looked angry. A small servant boy ran up to the great man and bowed low before him.

"My dog! Now!" the man roared.

"Dog not here yet," the boy began in faltering English, "he still..."

Without waiting for further explanation, the man lifted his foot and kicked the boy to one side.

"How dare you!
Out of my way!"
he said, and
strode on.
Lucy gasped.
She had seen
people be rude
to servants
before, she had
heard her
father shout
at them, but she
had never seen
anyone actually
kicked. She ran
to help the
boy up, but her mother restrained her.

"Don't, dear," she said. "Your actions
might be misunderstood. That's Sir Oswald...
I'm afraid he's got rather a temper."

"Sir Oswald!" Lucy said. "The man I'm to give flowers to?"

Her mother nodded. "Well he doesn't deserve them," Lucy said.

"He's perfectly hateful!"

"Sssh, dear!" Lucy's mother said, and was thankful when Lucy's ayah arrived to take her away. Lucy, inwardly still fuming about Sir Oswald's behaviour, allowed herself to be led off into one of the inner rooms to meet the children of other families visiting that day. Things were so busy, though, that when, looking outside, she saw the servant boy who'd been kicked by the horrible Sir Oswald, it was quite easy to give her ayah the slip.

She set off, down corridors and stairs,
to find him.

The boy was sitting, looking rather
miserable, on some steps in the splendid
back garden of the palace. He scrambled

to his feet when he saw
Lucy, looking
alarmed, and
began to bow.
Lucy saw that
he had a
large bruise
to the side
of his head.
"Please!
Don't do that,"
she said to him.
"I don't want
anything. I've only come to talk to you."
His eyes widened in panic. No member
of the raj ever talked to him. They
commanded him, shouted at him and
bullied him – they didn't talk to him.

"I think Sir Oswald was really horrible
to you – in front of everyone, too!"

Lucy burst out. "Have you worked for him for long?"

The boy was silent for a long while and Lucy had to repeat the question. She also added, "My mother and father aren't very nice to their servants, but they wouldn't dream of hitting them." Then she said, "What's your name? Mine's Lucy."

"My name is Aliph," the boy said nervously.

"And you are Sir Oswald's servant?"

The boy shook his head shyly. "I am his dog's servant."

Lucy gave a squeal of amazement. "His dog's servant?"

The boy nodded. "I walk his excellency's dog, groom it, feed it." He looked at the ground, "The dog was not quite ready when Sir Oswald wanted it."

"Oh, for goodness's sake!" Lucy said.

"Is he always like that? Always horrible?"
The boy nodded furtively. "Everything has
to be just so. He is – how do you say? –
irritated by things.
He suffers from
the heat, from
insect bites and
rashes. He has to
have all his clothes
sent from England.
He only eat
English food."

"Well, I know
how he feels,"
Lucy said, "but
that's no excuse
for being horrible
to people. If you
ask me, he needs
to be taught a lesson."

"What sort
of lesson do
you mean?"
Aliph asked.

"Like the lessons
in English I get from
the cook?"

"No. I mean something should happen
to him," Lucy said thoughtfully.
"Something that is not very nice."

"He fall off his horse?" Aliph said.
"He get given a very hot curry which burn
his mouth?"

Lucy shook her head. "If we did that,
then the cook would get in trouble. No, it's

got to be cleverer than that." Just then,
Lucy's ayah hurried down the steps,
calling to her.

"Whatever you doing, Miss Lucy?"
she said in a shrill, shocked voice.
"You come in straight away.
Your mother is asking for you."
Lucy was hauled to her feet and
her hair was tidied,
her dress smoothed,
her sash
straightened to the
ayah's satisfaction.

"There," the
ayah said, "now
you presentable."
She looked
sternly at the boy.
"You must not
talk to servants,

Miss Lucy."

"We had something to discuss,"
Lucy said, and she winked at Aliph as she
was led away. "Leave it to me!" she called
over her shoulder.

4

Red Hot Roses

Lucy, sitting in one of the vast reception rooms at Government House and waiting for her lift to the picnic, inspected her arms. Her prickly heat had gone down a little, she was pleased to see – she could go for ten minutes at a time without scratching now. She got up, stretched, and went to look into the garden, hoping she might see Aliph.

It was easy to look into the garden from this particular room, because the sliding doors had been opened and an artificial fence made of woven grasses put up. This was dampened down by the servants

spraying water on it, and now they were
fanning air through it. It was supposed to
feel like an cool breeze coming across an
English field, although Lucy didn't think it
did. All the guests had eaten a vast lunch
of fifteen courses. Some of the food had
been good, and some indifferent, for
several of the guests had brought their own
cooks with
them.

This might have been all right, except that

these cooks, instead of being allowed to prepare their own local dishes, were ordered to cook roast beef and Yorkshire puddings, and meat stews with dumplings. Such strange foreign foods were not understood by some of the Indian chefs.

After lunch, in the heat of the day, most of the visitors had taken a snooze. After that the party moved – by foot, by elephant and by carriage – to the centre

of Delhi to hear the proclamation read
by Lord Lytton. As he finished with the
promise that "Her Majesty's Indian
subjects are ever assured of their ruler's
protection and goodwill!" the people
cheered, guns boomed, military music
played and the regiments of soldiers cried
"Hoorah!" and "God save the Queen!"

Lucy, who'd been squashed into a small
space at the back of one of the stands, had
watched the celebrations eagerly – but also
kept her eye on Sir Oswald and noticed
him clip the ear of an
ayah and cuff a servant
round the head.

Oh yes, he certainly needed a lesson or two!
By the time the party returned to
Government House for tiffin, which was

like an English high tea, Lucy had decided
what to do about nasty Sir Oswald. When
the men went off on the tiger hunt, taking
beaters and servants and dogs, Lucy crept
away, went down to the kitchens and found
a small drum of dried
chilli powder. This she hid in
her little silk bag.

It was still hidden there an hour later as
Lucy and her mother, swaying precariously
in a little decorated cubicle on top of an
elephant, made their way to the picnic spot.

"This is a picnic and a half!" Lucy said
to her mother, looking back to the great
line of Lord Lytton's guests making

their way on elephants and camels towards
the river.

Her mother sighed. "Picnics used to be
you, me and your brother sitting on a rug in
the garden," she said. "And now look..."

Lucy could hardly believe the sight
before them at the riverside. Tents had been

erected in long rows, with lamp-posts
outside so that it looked like an
ordinary street.

Inside the tents, carpets had been laid,
and there were decorative hangings, vases
of flowers, pictures and tables and chairs.
In one of the larger tents there was even
a grand piano!

Lucy groaned quietly to herself as she was helped off her elephant. Now she'd have to start eating all over again!

❖

Three hours later, the men had returned from their hunt and everyone had eaten their fill. It was time for Lucy's big moment.

"At last," her mother said, "thank goodness you've managed to keep fairly clean all day." She spoke seriously to Lucy.

"Now, we've rehearsed this often enough. You have to..."

"I know!" Lucy said, "I wait for the other girl to give her flowers, then I go up onto the platform, give Sir Oswald my posy, drop a deep curtsey and walk backwards out of his presence."

"Don't let me down," said her mother. "Do smile nicely at him – and don't scratch your arms!"

"Of course not," Lucy said, looking thoughtfully at the red and white roses – flowers of India and England united. As Lucy made her way to the platform, her mother noticed that she seemed to be adjusting the petals and leaves, and was pleased she was taking such an interest. Thank goodness, too, that she seemed to have forgotten her instant dislike of Sir Oswald!

On the platform, before hundreds of people, the other girl presented her posy to

Lord Lytton, curtseyed and went off. It was Lucy's turn. Smiling sweetly, she handed over her posy to Sir Oswald. As she did so she murmured, "They do smell beautiful." This, she thought, would encourage him to sniff them! She then curtseyed low and backed off the platform.

Before she'd even got back to where her mother was sitting there was a tremendous sneeze from Sir Oswald.

Then another and another. Soon the great man was quite stricken with so many gigantic sneezes that it was all he could do to keep upright on his feet.

"Whatever's the matter with him?" Lucy's mother cried.

Lucy looked innocent.

"He gets allergies, I think," she said. "Maybe something in the bouquet doesn't agree with him."

Sir Oswald carried on sneezing – gigantic, elephant-sized sneezes which put

him flat on his back and
at last meant he had to go back to
Government House early.

"Oh dear," Lucy said. "He's going to
miss all the fireworks."

"Yes, jolly bad show," said her father
absently.

Jolly good show, Lucy thought to
herself as a magnificent display of
fireworks started and a shower of brilliant
stars lit up the night sky. It had certainly

been a day to remember – and she didn't
think Sir Oswald was going to forget it in
a hurry, either...

Notes

A Little Bit of History

In the mid-1770s, there wasn't a strong central power in India, and the East India Company (which had been set up to trade with India and the Far East in the 1600s) took advantage of this. With its armies, it gained control over much of India. In 1858, after rebellion by some of the Indian people, the British government took over from the East India Company. From then on, though, the Indian people made frequent attempts to gain independence, and this finally happened under their great leader, Gandhi, in 1947.

The British raj

This story is set during the time of the British raj (the word raj means ruler). In 1876, it was still thought that the Indians could not rule themselves properly, that they needed the British there to help. The proper word for this is "colonialism". The British did much that was good, however – they built railroad, telegraph and telephone systems,

and developed a system of food relief to help the Indian people through famines.

Slaves and Servants

It is thought that the British sometimes exploited the Indian people's willingness to serve. They often treated their servants like naughty children and were rude and sometimes even violent towards them. It was very rare for an English child to be allowed to befriend an Indian one.

Home Sweet Home

The raj tried to make India as much like "home" as possible. This often meant they only ate food imported from England, wore English fashions, listened to English music and read English newspapers. Some boasted that they spent years in India without speaking to a single native Indian. Others, thankfully, loved India and quite a few stayed on after independence in 1947.

Sparks: Historical Adventures

ANCIENT GREECE
The Great Horse of Troy – The Trojan War
0 7496 3369 7 (hbk)   0 7496 3538 X (pbk)
The Winner's Wreath – Ancient Greek Olympics
0 7496 3368 9 (hbk)   0 7496 3555 X (pbk)

INVADERS AND SETTLERS
Boudicca Strikes Back – The Romans in Britain
0 7496 3366 2 (hbk)   0 7496 3546 0 (pbk)
Viking Raiders – A Norse Attack
0 7496 3089 2 (hbk)   0 7496 3457 X (pbk)
Erik's New Home – A Viking Town
0 7496 3367 0 (hbk)   0 7496 3552 5 (pbk)
TALES OF THE ROWDY ROMANS
The Great Necklace Hunt
0 7496 2221 0 (hbk)   0 7496 2628 3 (pbk)
The Lost Legionary
0 7496 2222 9 (hbk)   0 7496 2629 1 (pbk)
The Guard Dog Geese
0 7496 2331 4 (hbk)   0 7496 2630 5 (pbk)
A Runaway Donkey
0 7496 2332 2 (hbk)   0 7496 2631 3 (pbk)

TUDORS AND STUARTS
Captain Drake's Orders – The Armada
0 7496 2556 2 (hbk)   0 7496 3121 X (pbk)
London's Burning – The Great Fire of London
0 7496 2557 0 (hbk)   0 7496 3122 8 (pbk)
Mystery at the Globe – Shakespeare's Theatre
0 7496 3096 5 (hbk)   0 7496 3449 9 (pbk)
Plague! – A Tudor Epidemic
0 7496 3365 4 (hbk)   0 7496 3556 8 (pbk)
Stranger in the Glen – Rob Roy
0 7496 2586 4 (hbk)   0 7496 3123 6 (pbk)
A Dream of Danger – The Massacre of Glencoe
0 7496 2587 2 (hbk)   0 7496 3124 4 (pbk)
A Queen's Promise – Mary Queen of Scots
0 7496 2589 9 (hbk)   0 7496 3125 2 (pbk)
Over the Sea to Skye – Bonnie Prince Charlie
0 7496 2588 0 (hbk)   0 7496 3126 0 (pbk)
TALES OF A TUDOR TEARAWAY
A Pig Called Henry
0 7496 2204 4 (hbk)   0 7496 2625 9 (pbk)
A Horse Called Deathblow
0 7496 2205 9 (hbk)   0 7496 2624 0 (pbk)
Dancing for Captain Drake
0 7496 2234 2 (hbk)   0 7496 2626 7 (pbk)
Birthdays are a Serious Business
0 7496 2235 0 (hbk)   0 7496 2627 5 (pbk)

VICTORIAN ERA
The Runaway Slave – The British Slave Trade
0 7496 3093 0 (hbk)   0 7496 3456 1 (pbk)
The Sewer Sleuth – Victorian Cholera
0 7496 2590 2 (hbk)   0 7496 3128 7 (pbk)
Convict! – Criminals Sent to Australia
0 7496 2591 0 (hbk)   0 7496 3129 5 (pbk)
An Indian Adventure – Victorian India
0 7496 3090 6 (hbk)   0 7496 3451 0 (pbk)
Farewell to Ireland – Emigration to America
0 7496 3094 9 (hbk)   0 7496 3448 0 (pbk)

The Great Hunger – Famine in Ireland
0 7496 3095 7 (hbk)   0 7496 3447 2 (pbk)
Fire Down the Pit – A Welsh Mining Disaster
0 7496 3091 4 (hbk)   0 7496 3450 2 (pbk)
Tunnel Rescue – The Great Western Railway
0 7496 3353 0 (hbk)   0 7496 3537 1 (pbk)
Kidnap on the Canal – Victorian Waterways
0 7496 3352 2 (hbk)   0 7496 3540 1 (pbk)
Dr. Barnardo's Boys – Victorian Charity
0 7496 3358 1 (hbk)   0 7496 3541 X (pbk)
The Iron Ship – Brunel's Great Britain
0 7496 3355 7 (hbk)   0 7496 3543 6 (pbk)
Bodies for Sale – Victorian Tomb-Robbers
0 7496 3364 6 (hbk)   0 7496 3539 8 (pbk)
Penny Post Boy – The Victorian Postal Service
0 7496 3362 X (hbk)   0 7496 3544 4 (pbk)
The Canal Diggers – The Manchester Ship Canal
0 7496 3356 5 (hbk)   0 7496 3545 2 (pbk)
The Tay Bridge Tragedy – A Victorian Disaster
0 7496 3354 9 (hbk)   0 7496 3547 9 (pbk)
Stop, Thief! – The Victorian Police
0 7496 3359 X (hbk)   0 7496 3548 7 (pbk)
A School – for Girls! – Victorian Schools
0 7496 3360 3 (hbk)   0 7496 3549 5 (pbk)
Chimney Charlie – Victorian Chimney Sweeps
0 7496 3351 4 (hbk)   0 7496 3551 7 (pbk)
Down the Drain – Victorian Sewers
0 7496 3357 3 (hbk)   0 7496 3550 9 (pbk)
The Ideal Home – A Victorian New Town
0 7496 3361 1 (hbk)   0 7496 3553 3 (pbk)
Stage Struck – Victorian Music Hall
0 7496 3363 8 (hbk)   0 7496 3554 1 (pbk)
TRAVELS OF A YOUNG VICTORIAN
The Golden Key
0 7496 2360 8 (hbk)   0 7496 2632 1 (pbk)
Poppy's Big Push
0 7496 2361 6 (hbk)   0 7496 2633 X (pbk)
Poppy's Secret
0 7496 2374 8 (hbk)   0 7496 2634 8 (pbk)
The Lost Treasure
0 7496 2375 6 (hbk)   0 7496 2635 6 (pbk)

20th-CENTURY HISTORY
Fight for the Vote – The Suffragettes
0 7496 3092 2 (hbk)   0 7496 3452 9 (pbk)
The Road to London – The Jarrow March
0 7496 2609 7 (hbk)   0 7496 3132 5 (pbk)
The Sandbag Secret – The Blitz
0 7496 2608 9 (hbk)   0 7496 3133 3 (pbk)
Sid's War – Evacuation
0 7496 3209 7 (hbk)   0 7496 3445 6 (pbk)
D-Day! – Wartime Adventure
0 7496 3208 9 (hbk)   0 7496 3446 4 (pbk)
The Prisoner – A Prisoner of War
0 7496 3212 7 (hbk)   0 7496 3455 3 (pbk)
Escape from Germany – Wartime Refugees
0 7496 3211 9 (hbk)   0 7496 3454 5 (pbk)
Flying Bombs – Wartime Bomb Disposal
0 7496 3210 0 (hbk)   0 7496 3453 7 (pbk)
12,000 Miles From Home – Sent to Australia
0 7496 3370 0 (hbk)   0 7496 3542 8 (pbk)